For Tanya, who was full of light —D.C.

tiger tales
an imprint of ME Media, LLC
202 Old Ridgefield Road, Wilton, CT 06897
Published in the United States 2008
Originally published in Great Britain 2007
by Hodder Children's Books
a division of Hodder Headline Limited
Text copyright ©2007 David Conway
Illustrations copyright ©2007 Dubravka Kolanovic
CIP data is available
ISBN-13: 978-1-58925-073-4
ISBN-10: 1-58925-073-7
Printed in China

by
David Conway

Shine
Moon
Shine

Illustrated by
Dubravka Kolanovic

tiger tales

One
snowy night,
in a great big city,

the moon fell from the sky and
landed on top of a very tall building.
All the people in the neighborhood
tried to put the moon back into the
night sky, but every time they tried
the moon fell again.

That night a young boy named
Owen sat with the moon to keep
it company.

The moon liked Owen for his kindness
and told him why it had fallen out of the
night sky and why it did not want to return.

"It is so dark up there," the moon told Owen.
"It makes me feel lonely."

Owen wanted to help the moon, so the next morning he got up early and captured sunbeams in a bucket. And that night he carried them to the very tall building.

Owen climbed the stairs higher and higher. When he reached the very top, where the moon sat pale and low, he released the sunbeams into the inky sky.

When Owen was done, the dark night didn't look so dark anymore.

But the sunbeams didn't stay. As quickly as they had appeared, they melted away.

The next day Owen
found a box of old flashlights
and carried them to the very
tall building.

Again Owen climbed the stairs higher and higher, and when he reached the very top Owen filled the night with beacons of light.

When Owen was done, the dark night
didn't look so dark anymore.

But the beacons of light
began to wane
and slowly
grew dimmer.

Until one by one they all went out.

On the third day Owen found
a ladder and carried it to the
very tall building.

Once again Owen
climbed the stairs
higher and higher.
When he reached
the very top, Owen
pushed his hands
through the cold dark
night and made holes to
let the daylight in.

But the
holes in the
tender night
didn't stay
and slowly
began to
close until
the sky was
very dark
again.

Owen sat in the roof's cold
snow, sad that the night would
not have a moon and sad that the
moon would never have a home.

Tears fell from his eyes and
landed on the soft white snow.
They became cold, so cold that
they began to freeze.

When Owen noticed this, he stopped crying and picked up one of his frozen tears. As it glistened in the darkness, he had an idea.

Owen gathered up his frozen tears from the soft white snow

and threw them far and wide into the inky sky.

"If you go back home now," Owen said to the moon,

"you will never be lonely again."

The moon trusted Owen and slowly but surely sailed back up into the darkness.

Then Owen cried at the top of his voice,

"SHINE, MOON, SHINE!"

At Owen's words, the moon's bright beams poured into the frozen tears, filling them with such rich moonlight that they lit up the night in a spectacular display.

All the people in the neighborhood
cheered and sang and clapped and danced
as the moon illuminated a new night sky.

Because now the night didn't look so dark anymore, and thanks to Owen and his frozen tears...

the moon was never lonely again.